MOTORSPORTS MANIACS

MONSTER TRUCKS

HOT TOPICS

BY KATE MIKOLEY

Gareth Stevens PUBLISHING

Please visit our website, www.garethstevens.com. For a free color catalog of all our high-quality books, call toll free 1-800-542-2595 or fax 1-877-542-2596.

Cataloging-in-Publication Data

Names: Mikoley, Kate, author.
Title: Monster trucks / Kate Mikoley.
Description: New York : Gareth Stevens Publishing, [2020] | Series: Motorsports maniacs | Includes bibliographical references and index.
Identifiers: LCCN 2019001137| ISBN 9781538240908 (pbk.) | ISBN 9781538240922 (library bound) | ISBN 9781538240915 (6 pack)
Subjects: LCSH: Monster trucks--Juvenile literature. | Monster trucks--Competitions--Juvenile literature.
Classification: LCC TL230.15 .M53 2020 | DDC 629.223/2--dc23
LC record available at https://lccn.loc.gov/2019001137

First Edition

Published in 2020 by
Gareth Stevens Publishing
111 East 14th Street, Suite 349
New York, NY 10003

Designer: Sarah Liddell
Editor: Kate Mikoley

Photo credits: Cover, pp. 1, 11 Simon Bratt/Shutterstock.com; dirt background used throughout Yibo Wang/Shutterstock.com; tire mark texture used throughout Slay/Shutterstock.com; pp. 5, 19, 21, 25, 27 Anadolu Agency/Contributor/Anadolu Agency/Getty Images; p. 7 Wikibofh~commonswiki/Wikimedia Commons; p. 9 Bettmann/Contributor/Bettmann/Getty Images; p. 13 ANDREW CABALLERO-REYNOLDS/Staff/AFP/Getty Images; p. 15 Quinn Rooney/Staff/Getty Images Sport/Getty Images; p. 17 Barry Salmons/Shutterstock.com; p. 23 Pavel L Photo and Video/Shutterstock.com; p. 29 Chris Ryan - Corbis/Contributor/Corbis Sport/Getty Images/

Printed in the United States of America

CPSIA compliance information: Batch #CS19GS: For further information contact Gareth Stevens, New York, New York at 1-800-542-2595.

CONTENTS

ALL ABOUT THE ACTION

If you've ever seen a **pickup truck** with extra-large tires, you've likely seen a monster truck. But if you've never been to a monster truck show, you might not know how much action these **vehicles** can get into!

TEST DRIVE

MONSTER TRUCK SHOWS ARE USUALLY OFF-ROAD EVENTS. THIS MEANS THEY TAKE PLACE ON DIRT TRACKS.

MONSTER TRUCK HISTORY

A man named Bob Chandler likely invented the first monster truck in the 1970s. Whenever his pickup truck needed to be fixed, he would make it a little bigger. He kept adding bigger tires. Finally, he had a truck with 5.5-foot (1.7 m) tires!

TEST DRIVE

BOB CHANDLER'S TRUCK, CONSIDERED BY MANY TO BE THE FIRST MONSTER TRUCK, WAS NAMED BIGFOOT!

In the 1980s, Chandler started using Bigfoot to **entertain** people. The big truck could drive over cars and even squash them! Soon more people had monster trucks. They started racing against each other and appearing in shows.

TEST DRIVE

IN THE EARLY DAYS OF MONSTER TRUCKS, THE SHOWS WERE OFTEN HELD DURING TRACTOR-PULLING EVENTS. TRACTOR PULLING IS A MOTORSPORT IN WHICH TRACTORS PULL A HEAVY LOAD.

Soon, there were so many monster truck fans that they started to get their own events. These took place all over the United States. People packed the stands to see drivers in huge trucks complete shocking **stunts**.

TEST DRIVE

IN EARLY EVENTS, MONSTER TRUCKS DROVE MUCH SLOWER THAN THEY DO TODAY, BUT THEY STILL PULLED OFF SOME UNBELIEVABLE FEATS, SUCH AS DRIVING UP ONTO OLDER CARS.

Today, one of the most well-known monster truck events is called Monster Jam. Trucks used in Monster Jams are about 10.5 feet (3.2 m) tall and 12.5 feet (3.8 m) wide! They weigh about 12,000 pounds (5,443 kg). That's as heavy as some elephants!

TEST DRIVE

TOGETHER, ONE MONSTER TRUCK WHEEL AND TIRE CAN WEIGH 645 POUNDS (293 KG)!

There are a few different kinds of events that happen at Monster Jams. In racing events, drivers try to complete a course as fast as they can. In these events, the driver who finishes the fastest is the winner.

TEST DRIVE

RACING IS MORE ABOUT SPEED THAN STUNTS, BUT THESE EVENTS CAN INCLUDE ACTION-PACKED JUMPS!

Monster Jams also have a few kinds of stunt events. In freestyle events, drivers have a certain amount of time to show off their best tricks. In two-wheel skills, drivers must lift at least two wheels off the ground.

TEST DRIVE

IN DONUT EVENTS, DRIVERS MUST MAKE THEIR MONSTER TRUCK SPIN AROUND IN A SMALL CIRCLE AS FAST AS THEY CAN.

BEING THE JUDGE

Racing events are timed, so most of the time it's pretty clear who won. Stunt events are judged. This means people choose who did the best tricks and pick the winner. At Monster Jams, the judges are often the people in the crowd!

TEST DRIVE

FOR SOME EVENTS, FANS CAN GO ON A WEBSITE AND CHOOSE A SCORE FOR EACH TRUCK. THE TRUCK THAT HAS THE HIGHEST **AVERAGE** SCORE IS THE WINNER.

PRACTICE MAKES PERFECT

Many Monster Jam drivers started out doing another motorsport, but that's not always the case. Monster Jam has a training program, or plan, called Monster Jam University. Drivers learn about safety and practice on courses like those in real Monster Jams.

TEST DRIVE

AFTER FINISHING THE TRAINING, SOME OF THE DRIVERS GO ON TO TAKE PART IN REAL MONSTER JAMS.

TIP-TOP SHAPE

Monster trucks are known for being strong and destroying other things. With all the stunts they do, they can get pretty beaten up, too. There are people whose job it is to fix the trucks and make sure they're in top working shape.

TEST DRIVE

MANY MONSTER TRUCKS HAVE THEIR OWN **UNIQUE** LOOK, BUT INSIDE THEY MOSTLY HAVE THE SAME PARTS. THIS MAKES IT EASIER FOR CREWS TO KNOW HOW TO FIX PROBLEMS.

A monster truck's tires can sometimes last for years. Other times they can be destroyed after just one event. It commonly only takes a few minutes for someone skilled in fixing monster trucks to change one of the huge tires.

TEST DRIVE

THERE ARE ALSO PEOPLE IN CHARGE OF BUILDING THE COURSE. SOMETIMES A WHOLE NEW COURSE HAS TO BE BUILT IN JUST ONE NIGHT!

SAFETY FIRST

Safety is one of the most important parts of monster truck shows. Drivers wear special gear, such as a suit that **protects** them in case of fire. Trucks also have cages to protect drivers in case the trucks roll over or crash.

TEST DRIVE

IN MONSTER JAMS, EACH TRUCK HAS THREE **FIRE EXTINGUISHERS** IN CASE THE TRUCK STARTS ON FIRE.

COOL TRUCKS

Many monster truck fans have favorite drivers. They also have favorite trucks. The trucks are often covered in colorful art. Some are even made to look like animals and have parts that look like teeth, ears, and tails!

TEST DRIVE

SMALLER TIRES ARE PUT ON MONSTER TRUCKS WHEN THEY'RE BEING MOVED SO THEY CAN FIT INSIDE THE VEHICLE CARRYING THEM.

MONSTER TRUCK SAFETY TIPS

MONSTER TRUCK DRIVERS SHOULD:

- MAKE SURE THE TRUCK IS WORKING PROPERLY BEFORE THE START OF THE EVENT.
- KNOW AND FOLLOW ALL THE RULES OF THE SHOW.
- WEAR SAFETY GEAR SUCH AS A HELMET, HEAD AND NECK PROTECTION, AND FIREPROOF CLOTHING.

MONSTER TRUCK FANS SHOULD:

- STAY IN THE ALLOWED AREAS. SOME AREAS NEAR THE FRONT ARE BLOCKED OFF FOR SAFETY REASONS.

FOR MORE INFORMATION

BOOKS

Abdo, Kenny. *Monster Truck Rallies*. Minneapolis, MN: Abdo Zoom, 2019.

Doeden, Matt. *Monster Trucks*. North Mankato, MN: Capstone Press, 2019.

Levit, Joe. *Motorsports Trivia: What You Never Knew About Car Racing, Monster Truck Events, and More Motor Mania*. North Mankato, MN: Capstone Press, 2018.

WEBSITES

Are Monster Trucks Scary?
wonderopolis.org/wonder/are-monster-trucks-scary
Find out more about monster trucks here.

Monster Jam 101
monsterjam.com/en-US/monster-jam-101-2
Read all about this action-packed event on Monster Jam's official website.

Publisher's note to educators and parents: Our editors have carefully reviewed these websites to ensure that they are suitable for students. Many websites change frequently, however, and we cannot guarantee that a site's future contents will continue to meet our high standards of quality and educational value. Be advised that students should be closely supervised whenever they access the internet.

GLOSSARY

average: a number found by adding numbers together and dividing the total by the amount of numbers added

entertain: to do things that are interesting for people to watch or listen to

fire extinguisher: a tool used to put out fires

pickup truck: a small truck with an open back that has low sides

protect: to keep safe

stunt: a difficult or dangerous action

unique: one of a kind

vehicle: an object that moves people from one place to another, such as a car

INDEX